VISIT AMAZON.COM FOR MORE
LITTLE HEDGEHOG BOOKS

I know my Nanny loves me. She shows me in so many ways!

She helps me brush my teeth. She wants me to be healthy!

Nanny takes me to the library to check out good books.

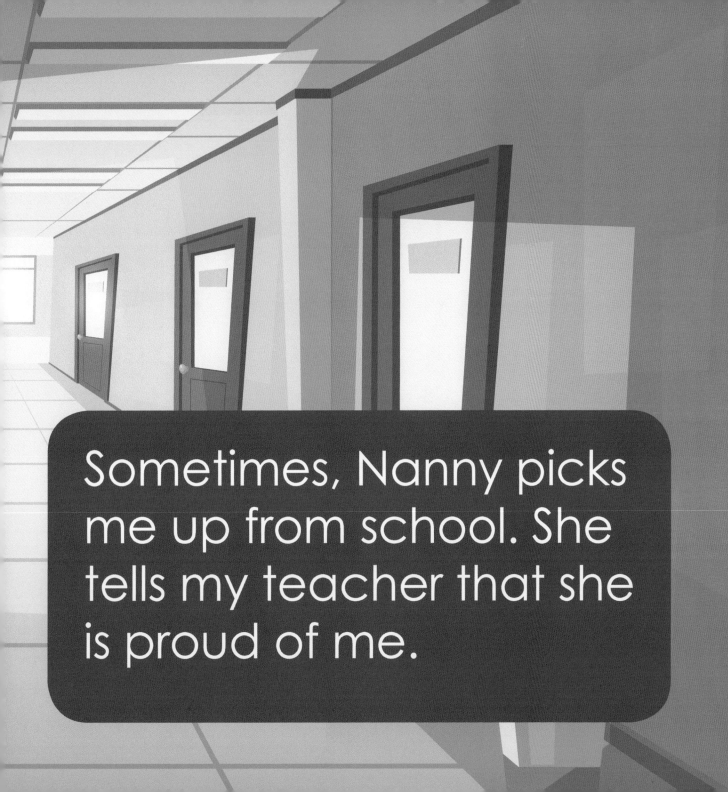

Sometimes, Nanny picks me up from school. She tells my teacher that she is proud of me.

Nanny likes to take me grocery shopping. (And sometimes, I get a treat.)

Nanny and I feed ducks in the park.

My Nanny takes me on lots of fun outings!

Nanny likes to take me to the playground to play.

When it is autumn, we go look at the pretty leaves together.

Even when Nanny is very busy, she makes time to talk to me.

In winter, she makes sure that I am bundled up warmly.

At Christmastime, we look at the twinkling lights together.

And when I am far away, I know that my Nanny thinks about me and misses me.

Printed in Great Britain
by Amazon

42010845R00021